This book
belongs to

....

For Sarah

FREDERICK WARNE

Published by the Penguin Group
Penguin Books Ltd, 80 Strand, London WC2R 0RL, England
Penguin Young Readers Group, 345 Hudson Street,
New York, New York 10014, U.S.A.
Penguin Books Australia Ltd, 250 Camberwell Road, Camberwell,
Victoria 3124, Australia
Canada, India, New Zealand, South Africa

4

ISBN-13: 978-0-723-25773-8
ISBN-10: 0 7232 5773 6

Printed in Great Britain

Lavender's Midsummer Mix-up

by Kay Woodward

Welcome to the Flower Fairy Garden!

Where are the fairies?
Where can we find them?
We've seen the fairy-rings
They leave behind them!

Is it a secret
No one is telling?
Why, in your garden
Surely they're dwelling!

No need for journeying,
Seeking afar:
Where there are flowers,
There fairies are!

Contents

Chapter One
Party Petals

"Phew!" Lavender heaved a huge sigh of relief and flopped down on a mossy hillock. She'd had the busiest—and best—week ever, getting ready for tomorrow's Midsummer Party, and everything was nearly done.

Lavender had the strangest of hobbies. While some Flower Fairies liked to help by stirring nutshells of fairy nectar or stringing garlands of honeysuckle and forget-me-not from branch to branch and twig to twig, she was at her happiest when up to her elbows in sparkling soapsuds.

On Monday, Lavender had scurried about the Flower Fairy Garden, reminding everyone about the Midsummer Party. Then she went back to her own beautiful flower and waited below its fragrant petals.

Soon, there was a long queue of Flower Fairies lining up to see her, each clutching a dirty, crumpled outfit and wearing an anxious smile.

"Is there anything at all you can do?" asked Elder tentatively, handing over a bundle of frothy lace that looked as if it had been dipped in mud.

"Hmm…" Lavender peered closely at the

delicate frock. "It'll take a hefty sprinkling of fairy magic…" She glanced up at worried-looking Elder and smiled. "But it'll be as good as new."

"Oh, thank you," breathed the little fairy, who was just as beautiful as her dress.

Next came Sycamore, who was well known for his treetop gymnastics. Lavender wasn't surprised to see that his leafy jacket and amber shorts were ripped to shreds. Again. Sycamore winked cheekily at Lavender, who tutted and dropped his rags on top of Elder's dress.

"Next!" she said briskly, wondering where

she had put her thistle needle and dandelion thread.

By Tuesday, the teetering pile of party laundry had become taller than Lavender, and she couldn't help feeling slightly nervous about the huge task that loomed ahead. Shaking long, dark curls from her face, she collected tablets of her own special lavender soap.

Suddenly, the air filled with a snowy fluttering of wings, and Lavender looked up, first with surprise and then with delight, to see her best friends.

"You're here!" she exclaimed as the swarm of white butterflies enveloped her in a ticklish hug. Without even waiting to be asked, they zoomed toward the dirty clothes, and in seconds a very strange procession was winding its way toward the stream—first Lavender, then a bobbing row of petal bonnets, dainty shoes, and other assorted items of fairy clothing, each carried by a dazzling white butterfly.

"Thank you!" cried Lavender, as the butterflies waved good bye. She dunked the first garment into the clear water, catching a glimpse of yellow out of the corner of her eye. She knew that this was Iris, a sweet but shy fairy who lived at the water's edge.

Lavender didn't call out, knowing that Iris would venture over when she was ready.

* * *

By Wednesday, all the Flower Fairy party clothes had been rubbed and scrubbed and scrubbed and rubbed clean. And Lavender and Iris were firm friends.

"So you really, truly do *enjoy* doing this?" asked Iris, who was having great difficulty understanding the idea that Lavender did laundry for fun. Iris was a very pretty fairy. The sunlight made her glossy auburn hair look extra-shiny, while her glorious yellow dress simply shone.

Lavender shrugged dispiritedly. "I have no

choice, really," she said. "Not until the elves lift the wicked charm that binds me to a life of soap and—" Unable to keep a straight face for a second longer, she giggled loudly at Iris's horrified expression. "I don't suppose you're any good at hanging out clothes…?" she added quickly.

"Of course!" replied Iris, jumping down to the riverbank to lend a hand.

Politely, Lavender asked the spiders if they could provide the washing lines. They were happy to oblige and were soon reeling out lengths of glistening gossamer, which Lavender stretched from flower to flower. Soon, sparkling clean party petals were flapping gently on the lines.

* * *

On Thursday, instead of taking a day off
while the warm breeze dried the beautiful
outfits, Lavender had been busier than ever.

She realized that her stocks of lavender-
scented soap were running low and that
they'd be much in demand before the
Midsummer Party—the one event when

everyone wanted to smell extra-specially delicious.

She gathered together her ingredients: three hundred and sixty-five lavender petals, to make soap that would smell fragrant on every day of the year; a sprinkling of fairy dust, to make sure the soap made whatever it touched magically clean; and a buttercup filled to the brim with dew, to bind everything together.

Lavender dropped all of the ingredients into a beechnut shell and, using a long stem from her own flower, stirred vigorously until everything had dissolved. Then, she poured the mixture into tiny nutshell molds and left them to set. Nothing was wasted—even the leftover drops were used to make a beautiful scent for the lucky Flower Fairies to dab on their wrists.

* * *

On Friday morning, the rising sun had revealed a kaleidoscope of dazzling color. Row upon row of fine garments, made from the prettiest petals, leaves, berries, and seeds that the Flower Fairy Garden had to offer, billowed in the breeze.

"Do you know what?" said Iris thoughtfully, "if you squint a bit, you can't see the purply-red stain on Elderberry's frock at all."

Lavender was shocked. How could she have let this happen? She'd been so careful! She tore across the grass, skidding to a halt before Elderberry's spotless dress... and heard Iris giggling gleefully behind her.

"Only teasing!" called Iris, delighted to have caught Lavender out.

That'll teach me, thought Lavender with a chuckle.

And now that everything really was clean,

there was one finishing touch for Lavender
to make. She picked a stem from her own
flower—one with a plump cluster of flowers
at its tip—and shook it near the billowing
outfits, releasing tiny spikes of lavender
laden with her own special fragrance.

* * *

Somehow, Lavender had drifted off to sleep. She creaked open her tired eyelids and sat upright on the mossy hillock. It was still Friday.

She looked to make sure that the party outfits were still there. They were. She glanced at the dandelion clock nearby. Its huge downy head was still half-full of floaty seeds, which meant that there was plenty of time before she had to gather and fold the clothes for tomorrow's party.

Like a jack-in-the-box, Lavender sprang to her feet. Then, she cupped her hands around her mouth and bellowed loudly, in a most unfairylike way. "Lavender's blue, diddle diddle!"

They were strange words indeed for a Flower Fairy who'd always considered her flower to be lilac, mauve, or—when the sun had set—deepest purple, but according to ancient fairy tradition, this color had always been known as "blue". And it didn't really matter to Lavender, because she knew that whatever color anyone thought it was, her flower would always smell as sweet.

Chapter Two
Time for Fairy Fun!

In a flash, a cloud of bees swarmed toward Lavender. Distracted for a moment by the party clothes, they wove in and out of the gossamer washing lines, nuzzling the fragrant petals. "Bzzzzzz…" they said approvingly.

Hot on their heels were the butterflies, who alighted playfully on Lavender's shoulders, whispering secrets of the world beyond the Flower Fairy Garden to her.

A dandelion seed floated past Lavender's nose, reminding her that time was passing and spurring her into action. "Let's play a game!" she said to her hovering, dancing audience. "Hide-and-seek?"

The bees hummed happily, while the butterflies flapped their wings in agreement.

"So who'll be…?" Lavender realized that she was speaking to thin air—"it," she finished. "Looks like it'll be me, then." But, like all the other Flower Fairies in the garden, she was an obliging creature, who so loved to take part in any game that she didn't mind which part she played. She ran lightly toward the nearest flower bed, fluttering into the air with excitement every few steps.

Spotting that the snapdragons were trembling suspiciously, she crept closer and peered inside. Sure enough, the bees had

dived into the cushiony
yellow blossoms, where
they were busy sampling
the delicious nectar.

"You're it!" sang
Lavender.

There was a single lazy
buzz by way of reply, and
it dawned on her that hide-
and-seek might not be the
best game to play with a
swarm of thirsty bees...

When it was Lavender's turn to hide, she knew just the place—among the petals of her very own flower! With her lovely lilac dress she would blend right in, and surely no one would dream that she'd hide here. It was just too obvious!

So she shook her wings, took a deep breath, and—with a sparkling burst of Flower Fairy magic—flew right to the tallest stems of lavender. And she might be hiding there still, if a troublesome leaf hadn't tickled her nose.

'Aaa … Aaa … Achoo!' she sneezed, and was discovered immediately by a passing butterfly.

The butterflies had thought of an extra-clever hiding place. They darted past the white narcissus, ignoring wild bindweed in the nearby hedge, and pretended to be pretty white dresses dancing on the washing line!

"Be careful!" warned Lavender, who had been keeping a nervous eye on her precious laundry. But the butterflies told her not to worry. They knew just how long it had taken her to make everything so clean, and they weren't going to spoil it.

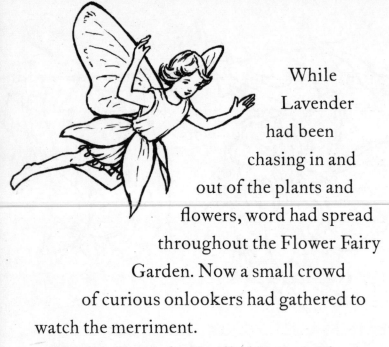

While
Lavender
had been
chasing in and
out of the plants and
flowers, word had spread
throughout the Flower Fairy
Garden. Now a small crowd
of curious onlookers had gathered to
watch the merriment.

"Hello, Lavender!" called Periwinkle, a
flaxen-haired fairy dressed in a dusky blue
tunic and sage green leggings. "Room for
one more?"

"Of course!" puffed Lavender, leaning
against a sturdy geranium stalk to catch her
breath.

"May I?" added Fuchsia. At Lavender's
nod, she performed a neat pirouette,
sending her pink and purple

petticoats spinning outwards.

"And me?" Zinnia—who was always brimming with energy—flapped her beautiful butterfly wings and fluttered to join them.

It had to be the best morning ever. They played tag and leapfrog. They raced one another. Then Lavender had a brainstorm— the Flower Fairy Garden was a ready-made obstacle course! So they chased one another around bushes, and leaped over streams. It was just what everyone needed after a week of party preparations.

"Look at me!" cried Periwinkle as he looped-the-loop around a climbing plant laden with pink and lilac flowers.

"Shhhhh!" hushed Sweet Pea from a leafy perch. She raised a finger to her lips and pointed to a cluster of flowers where baby Flower Fairy Sweet Peas were snoozing. "You'll wake the little ones!"

"Ooops!" whispered Periwinkle. "Sorry about that!" He rocketed back down to the garden, landing with a thud.

Lavender winced. "Be careful," she said. "You won't be able to dance at the Midsummer Party with a sprained ankle." She turned back to the obstacle course, spying Zinnia and Fuchsia weaving in and out of the tulips.

The ground shook.

"Periwinkle," Lavender said automatically, "whatever you're doing, be sure to take care."

"Huh?" said Periwinkle.

Lavender turned to see him sitting cross-legged on the bare earth, snacking on a ripe hazelnut. The ground shook again, louder now. Whoever or whatever was making the thudding noise, it wasn't Periwinkle. So, gathering all her courage, Lavender bravely peeped around a prickly hawthorne bush and caught her breath at what she saw…

Strolling over the lawn toward them were two human children, so tall that they blocked out the sun. The loud noise was the sound of a huge black-and-white ball that they were bouncing as they walked. Thud! Thud-thud!

Lavender shrank back into the shadows of the hawthorne bush, accidentally pricking herself on a spike and then muffling the squeak of pain in case they heard her.

"Sam, what's that?" said a girl with auburn hair, a dusting of freckles, and a heart-shaped face. "I'm sure I saw something twinkle. Do you think it could be a fairy...?"

Her heart sinking, Lavender patted the folds of her petal dress, realizing instantly that her precious handful of fairy dust that she kept for emergencies was gone. The girl must have spotted it shining in the grass.

"Let's go and investigate!" said the other child, a boy with ruffled blond hair. "Hurry up, Milly!"

And, curious eyes fixed firmly on the ground, they crept straight toward the bottom of the garden—and the Flower Fairies.

Chapter Three

Visitors

Lavender thought back quickly over the
Flower Fairy Law that every fairy was
taught as soon as they were old enough…
Humans—especially children—were
known to be very inquisitive creatures,
who had long suspected that fairies lived
in their world. But if humans knew that
fairies really did exist, right under their
noses, the Flower Fairies' world would

be in danger
of discovery.
Which was why
they must stay out
of sight at all times.

It was time for a real-life game of hide-and-seek. Keeping under cover of the shadowy bushes, Lavender tiptoed over to where the other Flower Fairies were huddled beneath a large, leafy plant.

"Wait until you hear my splendid plan," said Periwinkle, who wasn't scared of anything. "Hiding under this—" he snapped off a dark green leaf— "I can smuggle all the Flower Fairies to safety, one by one." He looked proudly around the group as if expecting a round of applause.

"That really is a splendid plan," said Lavender, careful not to hurt his feelings, "but it's a little risky. The human children will be suspicious of anything and everything that moves."

"Ah, yes," said Periwinkle, nodding sensibly. "So what do you suggest?"

"We must hide," said Lavender. Quickly,

she told her fairy friends to find a hiding place and stay there—no matter how close the humans came. Most importantly, they must stay absolutely still.

So the Flower Fairies stole away. No one dared to fly, in case their gossamer wings were spotted shining in the afternoon sunlight.

* * *

"Do you think we're close?" whispered Milly, so loudly that the Flower Fairies—who have incredible hearing—could hear her right at the bottom of the garden.

Despite her fear, Lavender chuckled to herself. If only humans realized just how much noise they made, they might guess why fairies were so hard to find.

"The fairies are listening to us now…" said Sam in a spooky voice. "They're hiding under this very bush." Without warning, he reached down toward the hawthorne branches where Lavender had hidden, and swept them aside. "Boo!" he said. Then, "Ouch!", as he found out how prickly it was.

Lavender sped away. While she'd been listening to the children, a plan had begun to form in her mind—an ingenious plan that would keep Flower Fairy Garden safe and keep the human children happy. But first,

she had to talk to the bees and butterflies.
She glanced over her shoulder as huge, shiny
shoes stomped into view. Faster—she must
go faster!

The bees had supped the nectar from the
snapdragon flowers and were now buzzing
lazily nearby, full after their sticky feast.

"Hi, Snapdragon!" Lavender waved to the

fairy snuggled comfortably between the blossoms. "Stay out of sight—there are humans around!" Snapdragon nodded and nestled farther into the flowery depths.

Lavender scampered quickly toward the bees, wishing for the thousandth time that she hadn't lost her fairy dust. And it took such a long time to make too…

Each Flower Fairy gathers pollen from their own flower, then grinds it between two rough stones until all that remains is a heap of tiny glittering particles—fairy dust. The precious dust can be used for all sorts of magical things—for summoning friendly insects and for distracting humans with its alluring sparkle. It can even be used to decorate flowers at Christmas time.

Luckily, the bees had seen Lavender, and they buzzed toward her when she called. The white butterflies came too—they had been visiting Lavender's own flowers nearby, fluttering merrily around the fragrant petals. Quickly, the Flower Fairy whispered her idea, before hurrying across to speak to Honeysuckle.

* * *

The children were really close now,
wriggling their way between overgrown
bushes and tripping over tree roots.
Occasionally, Sam would dart out a hand to
lift a smooth pebble or to examine an old,
crumbling garden ornament.

"We're never going to find anything,"
sighed Milly, looking wistfully at a mass of
elegant roses—unwittingly overlooking the
tiny fairy huddled beneath one of the flowers,
her soft pink dress and wings exactly the
same color as the rose itself.

Lavender too had concealed herself
among her own
flowers. And
as she peered
around the
garden, her keen
fairy eyes—so
much sharper than

human eyes
—saw that the
other Flower
Fairies had
done the same
thing, their outfits providing
the perfect camouflage to fool
curious children.

Milly and Sam thudded
closer and closer, until they
were so near that she could
almost touch them. A twig
snapped beneath Sam's foot,
as if signalling to Lavender
that this was the moment to set her plan
in motion. She nodded at Honeysuckle,
who was balanced high on his wild,
raggedy flower, swaying slightly in the
breeze. He blew his flowery horn loudly.
Toot!

Milly frowned, almost as if she'd heard Honeysuckle's tiny signal, but a buzzing crowd of bees distracted her at once. They swarmed noisily into the air, where a host of white butterflies joined the throng, flitting and fluttering around crazily, like handkerchiefs waving in the distance.

Then, at another toot from Honeysuckle's trumpet... they were off! The bees and butterflies leaped from flower to flower,

pausing for a moment by the trickling stream, before continuing their merry Midsummer dance around the garden.

Eagerly, the children followed, not realizing that they were being led farther and farther away from the Flower Fairies' secret world.

"Fairies at the bottom of the garden?" gasped Sam as he dashed headlong through the flower beds, kicking the ball before him. "Rubbish! We must have seen these pesky insects!"

Milly said nothing. But she stopped for a moment and looked back longingly at the multicolored array of flowers that they'd left behind. Then she rushed after Sam.

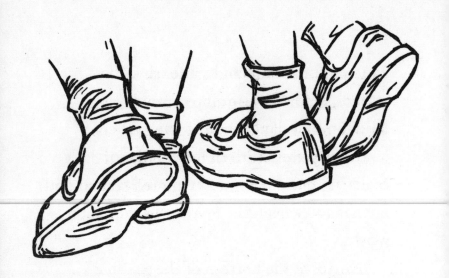

As the sound of children disappeared into the distance, an amazing transformation began to take place. The charming—if slightly overgrown—garden rustled and shook into life. Here, a dainty head peeped out of a crinkly yellow blossom. There, a tiny arm stretched from behind a stem where its owner had been hiding.

Leaves were pushed aside, petals unfolded, and long grasses moved to reveal a garden full of smiling Flower Fairies.

Lavender gazed around, thrilled that her plan had worked. But her relief turned swiftly to despair as her eyes met a dreadful sight.

She gulped, closed her eyes, and then looked again.

Oh no!

Chapter Four
Disaster!

Where the gently billowing rows of bright, clean party petals had once been, there was now only a tangled mess of gossamer and flowers.

As the children had rushed headlong after the bees and butterflies, they had snapped the delicate gossamer washing lines and trampled over the Flower Fairies' party outfits. Now all of the beautiful clothes lay on the ground, covered with mud, moss, and grass stains. Worse still, some were horribly torn.

For a moment, Lavender felt frozen to the spot. Then she sank to her knees, put her face into her hands, and sobbed.

Everything is my fault, she thought. *If only I hadn't played games earlier, I wouldn't have attracted the attention of the children... and then I wouldn't have had to dream up my stupid plan... and then the bees and the butterflies wouldn't have zoomed over the washing lines... and then the children wouldn't have stomped over the clothes.* Great fat tears slipped down her cheeks as she realized that

all of her hard work was ruined. And with no party outfits to wear, the Midsummer Party would be ruined too. If only she'd snoozed instead. If only…

Lavender listened to the cries of disappointment echoing all around. She hardly dared to look—everyone was certain to be upset and so disappointed with her. But cautiously, she lifted her head.

She needn't have worried. Everyone knew that Lavender wasn't to blame for the messy clothes. And they were such kindly creatures that they didn't blame the children either. After all, how were Milly and Sam to know that they'd been racing through a miniature laundry, when the Flower Fairies kept their world so secret?

"Don't worry," said Elder, handing Lavender a handkerchief made from her own lacy blossom.

"But everything's so d-d-dirty!" wept Lavender.

"Oh, that's not such a bad thing," said a small, exceedingly grubby little fairy, only recognizable because of the sycamore seeds he was attempting to juggle with. "If you're wearing dirty clothes, you can get up to heaps more fun!"

Sycamore's giggles were infectious,

and soon everybody was laughing—even Lavender. The Flower Fairies flocked around to comfort her, brimming with brilliant ideas and plans of action.

Periwinkle leapt on to a mushroom and cleared his throat importantly. "There's a whole day before the Midsummer Party," he announced. "That's plenty of time to get everything sorted. And we'll all lend a hand."

It was true. There was no shortage of offers to help. Flower Fairies darted here and there, collecting the clothes that had been scattered far and wide by the children's hasty feet. Carefully, Lavender examined every garment before sorting them into different piles: terribly filthy, quite dirty, slightly grubby, crumpled but clean, and absolutely spotless.

Lavender herself took charge of the "terribly filthy" pile, while advising other Flower Fairies on just the right amount of soap to use when cleaning their share of the party clothes.

There was one other sorry heap of petals —clothes that had been ripped so badly that a dunk in the stream would not fix them. And here, Tansy came to the rescue. With her tiny sewing kit—and a good helping of fairy dust—she mended rips and holes, neatened jagged edges, and replaced buttons and beads. Zinnia brought fresh petals for Tansy to patch the most ragged outfits.

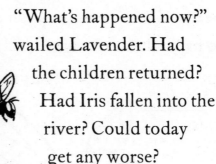

Suddenly, there was an agonized shout
from the stream, and all the Flower Fairies
flung down whatever they were doing and
ran to see what was amiss. The distressed
sound was coming from Iris, who had been
allocated a pile of slightly grubby clothes
to scrub and rinse.

"What's happened now?"
wailed Lavender. Had
the children returned?
Had Iris fallen into the
river? Could today
get any worse?

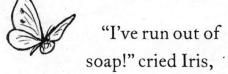

"I've run out of soap!" cried Iris, looking so sad that Elder began searching in her pockets for another hankie.

Lavender was so relieved that nothing worse was wrong, it took a moment for her to realize that this was quite a problem. Soap wasn't something that she could conjure up out of nowhere—it took time, effort, and an awful lot of ingredients.

But this time, the bees and butterflies rallied around. While Lavender searched for enough dew to fill a buttercup, they flitted here and there among the lavender flowers, collecting the petals and pollen that their Flower Fairy friend needed to make her special soap.

And so, for a second time, everything was washed and clean.

With so many creatures
helping, it was finished in
a twinkling. But things were
not destined to run smoothly in the
Flower Fairy Garden that afternoon. There
were no drying lines. Not a single one.

The spiders' delicate gossamer strands
had been snapped, tangled and ruined.
What little was left wasn't big enough to
hang a single fairy sock, never
mind an entire Midsummer
collection of clothes.
The spiders
had been
frightened

away by the
commotion and no
matter how softly
or sweetly Lavender
called, they were too
scared to return.

"If you will allow me," said
Periwinkle, bowing deeply in front of
the forlorn fairy, "I will amaze you with the
strong yet supple string I'll make from my
flower stalks, which just happen to be perfect
for washing lines. Are you watching…?"

Lavender was watching. And she was
definitely amazed.

The birds—who were quite a nosy bunch
—had been watching all the frenzied fairy
activity with interest. And when Rose and
Honeysuckle began hanging string between
the top stems of their plants, they could
resist no longer. As one, they dived down to
the garden to see what was going on.

"Perfect!" said Lavender, as the feathery
creatures landed gracefully beside her. She'd
soon realized that although

Periwinkle was
doing an
admirable job,
there was no
way he could
make enough
washing lines
to dry all the
clothes before
sundown.

"Here's
what I'd like
you to do," she said to the
birds.

They looked at one another curiously
and then looked back at the little Flower
Fairy, who picked a dripping-wet petal tunic
from the pile of clothes and handed it to the
first bird. "Would you fly as high as you
can and as fast as you dare until this is dry?"
Lavender asked. "Please?"

The obliging bird nodded. And soon,
the sky was fluttering with feathers and
petals. It was a beautiful sight. Lavender
paused for a moment to watch the whirl
of color, then looked down, down, down
at her checklist and heaved a great sigh.
Suddenly, the Midsummer Party seemed
as far away as ever...

* * *

If Lavender thought she'd had a busy week, it was nothing compared to her hectic Friday afternoon. She'd never had so much to do or so many people to look after. And she'd never had so much fun. Gradually, she began to forget that anything had gone wrong at all.

She masterminded the whole project, flitting here and there to make sure everything was running smoothly. Tansy was repairing torn and shredded clothes, cleverly using petals and leaves to cover the ripped edges.

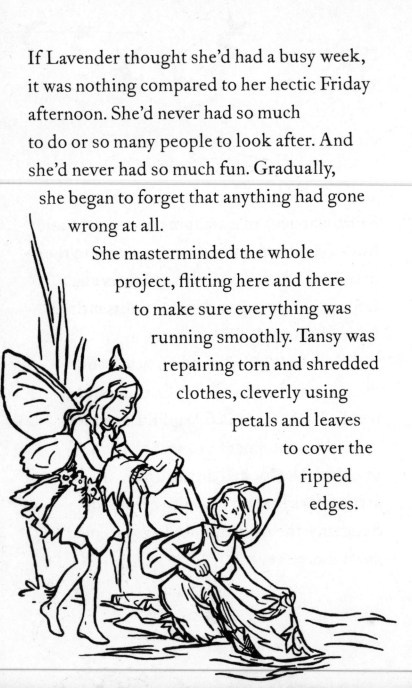

And no matter how closely Lavender looked, she was unable to spot where new petals had been sewn in place. Meanwhile, Iris was scrubbing extra hard at stubborn stains. Lavender skipped past, not forgetting to tell the hard-working fairy what a fine job she was doing, before helping to peg clean clothes on to Periwinkle's lines with bent twigs. Amongst the mayhem, she even managed to find a little time to make more fairy dust.

As the afternoon wore on, everyone began to tire.

"I'm pooped!" declared Periwinkle. He flopped down on a pillow of springy heather and mopped his brow. "I could easily go to… zzz…"

"Wake up!" said Lavender frantically. "There's still so much to do!" She tappety-tap-tapped Periwinkle's shoulder, until his eyes creaked open, but he immediately nodded off again.

"Can I help?" asked a singsong voice. It was Canterbury Bell—a blue-eyed fairy wearing a big purple hat, a pink shirt, and

shorts made from the same silvery gossamer as his wings. He held a bunch of bell-shaped purple blossoms, which he swung to and fro so that they chimed loudly.

"Me too!" added Ragged Robin, a Flower Fairy whose tattered outfit lived up to his name, and who was not often seen in these parts—his home was the wet marsh outside the garden. "I heard about the unfortunate events and came as soon as I could," he explained. "I thought a Midsummer melody might cheer everyone up." And he played a lively tune on his reed pipe.

The beautiful fairy music wafted around the garden, lifting everyone's spirits at once.

The garden was bathed in the warm, rosy glow of the setting sun as the birds dropped the last of their dry clothes into Lavender's open arms.

"Thank you!" she called as they fluttered back to their nests and perches. And tired, but happy to have helped, the Flower Fairies returned to their homes to rest before the Midsummer Party.

Tomorrow, it would be time to have fun, but now it was time to sleep. Lavender returned to her cozy bed. Most of the dainty lilac flowers were gone now, but she knew that new buds would appear soon. She laid down her sleepy head, to dream of lovely fairy friends who'd been so kind.

Chapter Five
Party Time

The next morning dawned bright and clear. Soon the Flower Fairy Garden was filled with beautiful birdsong.

It was the perfect wake-up call. Lavender opened her eyes, then stretched luxuriously. It was Midsummer's Day—the longest and most magical day of the year, and the day of the Midsummer Party. She could hardly wait!

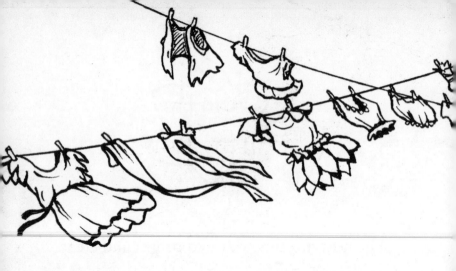

Lavender fluttered from her snuggly bed of leaves down to the green grass below and splashed her face with drops of sparkling dew.

"Now I'm ready for anything!" she announced to a passing ladybird, who flapped her spotted wings in reply.

Gathering a few last stems of Lavender from her plant and bundling them under her arm, the little lilac fairy strode purposefully toward the piles of clean party clothes and the petals still drying on Periwinkle's washing lines. For the second time that week,

she ran to and fro among the outfits, shaking
her delicate flowers all about. A gentle breeze
blew them here, there, and everywhere,
until even the air was fragrant. A musical
tinkling sound rushed through the garden,
and suddenly there was magic in the air, too,
making all the fairy petals sparkle and shine
even more than the day before.

Carefully, Lavender began to pluck
the clean clothes from the washing lines,
marvelling again at how wonderful they
looked. Soon, the pile was even taller
than her!

Lavender gently placed Elder's delicate lacy dress into her waiting arms. "Ta-daaaa!" she said proudly. There was not a mud spot to be seen.

"Oh, Lavender…" breathed the little Flower Fairy, fluttering her pale, creamy wings. "This is wonderful… However can I thank you?"

Lavender blushed as she thought of all the fairies who'd lent a hand. "I should be thanking you," she said. "Just make sure that you have a marvelous time." And, staggering slightly under her load, she hurried to meet her next satisfied customer.

"Excellent!" said Honeysuckle, admiring the extra petals that had been sewn on to the bottom of his shorts, to make them super-tough.

"Superb!" said Periwinkle, whose blue tunic had been sprinkled with fairy dust to give it a silvery sheen.

Rose was so pleased with her dainty pink frock that she was speechless.

At twelve noon precisely, Canterbury Bell's flowers began to ring merrily. It was the sound that everyone had been waiting for—the signal that the Midsummer Party was about to begin!

Dressed in their finery, the Flower Fairies skipped and danced toward a clearing in a secret corner of the garden. This was the fairy court—where the very best parties in all of Flower Fairyland took place.

Ooohs and aaahs of delight echoed through the garden as the fairies saw the mouth watering fairy feast that awaited them.

There were fairy cheeses made from Mallow's delicious seeds, piles of ripe hazelnuts, bowls of wobbly crab-apple jelly, and nutshells filled to the brim with

Elderberry's fragrant juice. The Flower Fairies piled their daisy plates high with food and dipped buttercups into the purple juice.

And then the dancing started. Honeysuckle, Canterbury Bell, and Ragged Robin provided the music, while Columbine, Almond Blossom, and Fuchsia—who needed no excuse to whirl and waltz—led the way on to the dance floor.

Lavender gazed at the dazzling jumble of color before her eyes. Everything had turned out splendidly. And everyone looked wonderful. She was having the best time!

"Excuse me?"

She looked down as a tiny Sweet Pea fairy tapped her on the knee. "Yes, my sweet?" she asked.

"I have to give you this," said the tiny fairy solemnly, handing her a scroll of fairy parchment.

Lavender's heart dropped like a stone in a very deep well. She untied the golden strands coiled around the parchment and unrolled it, her stomach turning to jelly as she did so. She gulped. The message was from the Queen of the Meadow and Kingcup. They wanted to see her—at once.

Anxious thoughts chased around Lavender's head like nervous butterflies. The king and queen must be angry with her for creating mayhem in the peaceful garden. Would they banish her from the Flower Fairy Garden…?

She went to find out.

Lavender tiptoed toward the King and Queen of the Flower Fairies, resplendent in their gorgeous royal robes. As she curtsied before them, she could not help but tremble.

"Why do you look so scared?" asked the Queen of the Meadow gently, her silky, golden hair glistening in the sunlight. She toyed with a string of olive-green pearls around her slender neck.

Lavender could not speak.

"We would like to thank you for your incredibly hard work," said Kingcup, a huge smile appearing on his handsome face. He looked around the assembled fairies, who were watching the meeting curiously. "At this time of year," he said, "Lavender becomes the most important fairy in the Flower Fairy Garden. Without her, the Midsummer Party clothes would be lackluster and dull and in some cases"—he winked at Honeysuckle—

"quite dirty. But with Lavender's efforts, everyone dazzles."

"Er... Your Kingship, sir," said Lavender, unable to stay silent. "It's thanks to all the Flower Fairies that this Midsummer Party has turned out so well this year." She curtsied apologetically.

"That is a very noble thing to say," said the Queen of the Meadow. "But even so, your contribution has been quite magnificent. And I'm sure everyone would agree."

There were deafening cheers, and Lavender blushed. She didn't think she'd ever been so proud—or so happy.

Each Midsummer Party it was traditional to reward one of the Flower Fairies by singing their special song. This year, the honor belonged, of course, to Lavender. And everyone—from the smallest Flower Fairy to the regal Kingcup—gathered round to sing:

"Lavender's blue, dilly dilly"—so goes
    the song;
All round her bush, dilly dilly, butterflies
throng;
(They love her well, dilly dilly, so do the
bees;)

While she herself, dilly dilly, sways in the breeze!

"Lavender's blue, dilly dilly, Lavender's green;
She'll scent the clothes, dilly dilly, put
    away clean—
Clean from the wash, dilly dilly, hanky
    and sheet;
Lavender's spikes, dilly dilly, make them
all sweet!"

Visit our Flower Fairies website at:

www.flowerfairies.com

There are lots of fun Flower Fairy games and
activities for you to play, plus you can find out more
about all your favorite fairy friends!

More tales from these Flower Fairies
coming soon!

Candytuft   Buttercup   Strawberry   Almond Blossom

Have you log...
the Flower Fairies™ Friends
Friendship Ring?

In the land of Fairyopolis every fairy is your friend
and now the Flower Fairies
want to share their secrets with you!

Online

Visit **www.flowerfairies.com**
and sign up for the Flower
Fairies Friendship Ring
and you will receive:

❀ Secret Fairy Coded Messages
❀ News and updates
❀ Invitations to special events
❀ Every new friend receives a
  special gift from the Flower Fairies!
  (while supplies last.)

Frederick Warne & Co.
A division of Penguin Young Readers Group